PEACE AND LOVE AND FEAR OF LIFE

Flash Fiction by

Guy Rowley

PEACE AND LOVE AND FEAR OF LIFE
Flash Fiction by Guy Rowley

Copyright © 2016 Guy Rowley

Published in the United States by Guy Rowley

ISBN (paperback): 978-0-9970838-0-4
ISBN (e-book): 978-0-9970838-1-1
Library of Congress Control Number: 2016902671

Cover design: Guy & Rebecca Rowley & Josh Pinkerman
Guy: facebook.com/peaceandloveandfearoflife
Rebecca: facebook.com/RebeccaRowleyActor
Josh: jpfineart@gmail.com

Cover and Interior Layout: Nick Zelinger, nzgraphics.com

Illustrations:
Cover portrait of the author, watercolor, 1970: Charlie Nelson
"The World" et al, pencil and photocopy: Guy and Rebecca Rowley
"Peace and Love and Fear of Life," multimedia: Josh Pinkerman
"Guy & Becky" photo: Russell Rowley

First Edition
Printed in the United States of America

FOR MOM

Mom, hear what I shall say, for it is true
That half of what's inside of me is you
And all these things you share with me, your boy.
If I am happy, greater is your joy.
If I am sad, half that is borne by you.
If I achieve, my pride expands by two.
If I should fail, your eyes make me the best.
I've felt your heart alive within my chest
And know your worth: I see you with the stars.
You are my best and closest, truest friend.
I'm yours.

ACKNOWLEDGMENTS

Sincere thanks to my family: Mom, Dad, Rob, Rick, Lorraine, Russell, Laurel Ann, Lynna, Ryan, Virginia, John, Robert, and Rebecca for their love, help and inspiration; Josh Pinkerman for his art and enthusiasm; Dr. Jana Johnson for her wise council; Kathryn Jordan for her editing; The Palm Springs Writer's Guild for a lot of things; and C.L. (Jim) Hoang for his heartening words and friendship.

See mulberryfieldsforever.com for a look at *Once Upon A Mulberry Field*, Jim's healing story of love and the Viet Nam War.

PEACE AND LOVE AND FEAR OF LIFE

CONTENTS

FOREWORD

SPECULATION

MYSTERY

ADVENTURE

PIONEERS

LOVE

FOREWORD

I went for a hike this morning wondering how to introduce and explain this collection of weird stories. This is what hatched.

TRUE STORY

I SAW A DRAGON today—maybe two. I was hiking near Cathedral City, California when I looked up from the trail and there it was. I had watched it fly for probably a full minute. It was all black with long, angular wings and a narrow stretched-out tail. I tried to tell myself it could be a frigate bird, but nah, what would a frigate bird be doing in the desert? It didn't look like a frigate bird, it looked like a *dragon*! The thing's tail was three or four feet long. The whole thing could have been over be eight feet.

I began to accept the dragon as a real part of the world—and when it turned a little in the air and looked like it might come towards me, I hoped it would. If it attacked me, it would be worth it. I wanted to know it. I wanted it to know me. Come closer dragon, I thought. Come closer.

It didn't come closer, but I wasn't disappointed. I'd gotten a good long look at the thing and it was still a dragon when it disappeared behind the hills. Maybe I was a little bit relieved.

About fifteen-minutes further up the trail, I saw another one. It could have been the same one, I don't know. It was perched on a ledge a long way off. The trail was headed toward it, and I sped up to try to get a closer look. The ledge went out of sight for a minute or two and when I got to where I could see it again the dragon was gone.

Later, on my way back down, I spooked a Bighorn out of a shady place on the trail. It ran out into the sun and down a hill, jumped the bottom of a gully and ran up the next hill to another patch of shade. It watched me for half-a-minute and then started nibbling at the brush. It was every bit as beautiful as the Dragons.

****

Peace and Love and Fear of Life is a collection of short stories and flash fiction mostly written between 2012 and 2015. In the same sense as the dragon story above, these stories are true. They are not conjured out of thin air. They are amalgams assembled from memories that have moved me—memories of experiences, characters, stories, dreams and imaginings. If something haunts me emotionally I pry into it, dig up related memories and glue them into a unique story with what-ifs. When the story itself moves me, I polish it up over time, trimming it to the essentials.

In most of these stories I explore *peace* and *love* as goals and *fear* as the motivator—the elicitor of action—the thumbtack on the chair. Is it fear that creates all drama: comic and tragic? Is it drama that creates empathy? Is it empathy that creates love? Where does beauty fit in? Is it love? Is beauty the love of awe? If a horse-and-half can eat a bale-and-a-half in a day-and-a-half, how many pancakes does it take to shingle a dog house: a stack-and-a-half? Why is everything a question? Everything is a gray area to me, that's why. So I can't defend a one-sided argument. Humor is the bail-out. It both illuminates and celebrates of the paradoxes. It's self-defense. True story.

Peace and Love.

17, JUNE 2015   PALM DESERT, CALIFORNIA

Hey, Peace and Love Generation: WE WON! We have the power. Ignore the fear merchants and actually look around you. The world is beautiful. The world wants tolerance, openness, healing—peace and love. Revel in it. Enable it. BE COOL—VOTE LOVE.

SPECULATION

FEAR OF LIFE

This is how it feels: like fear. This is how it tastes: like hunger. This is what you know: nothing. This is what you want: peace.

December

You may end up thinking I'm crazy, but I'm not. Neither am I schizophrenic nor hallucinatory. I am not a compulsive liar, nor do I even have an abnormally wild imagination. In those respects I am as normal as it is for you to end up thinking I'm crazy.

My theory (as I recall presenting it to a theatre of eminent neurologists and psychiatrists during the dissection of a cadaver's brain) is that I suffer from a syndrome composed of, firstly: a difficulty with the differentiation of dreams from reality, and secondly:

a marked increase in the incidence and acuity of fear. The syndrome is symptomatic of a cascading ischemic stroke affecting the "fight-or-flight" region of the back brain and the nearby hippocampus, specifically, the dream center in the ammon's horn—but I'm no doctor. My neurologist says I did have a small stroke and we need to run more tests. My psychiatrist says we have a lot of work to do.

I have learned that I am most afraid when there is nothing to be afraid of. If I am idle, the fear can strengthen to the point of being palpable to the odd sense or two, like tasting or touching The Void. Staying occupied is the only remedy. The more concerned I am, the less afraid I am. It is for that therapeutic effect that I am busying myself with this account.

As to memories and dreams, it seems to me that I can tell the difference—but I know I can't. Telling me that my memories and dreams are jumbled is like telling the colorblind person that the color he sees is wrong. Maybe he can see the logic in what you say, but he sees what he sees and it looks how it looks to him. Logic, if based on a flawed premise, can take you anywhere (witness politics and religion) and no premise is one-hundred percent unflawed. I don't trust logic anymore because I have a recurring dream in which I am earnestly told, as if it were somehow abnormal, that there are flawed premises locked into my mind.

It does no good to go round and round about it. All I want to do here is stay busy by recounting a few of my most pervasive memories. Your own premises and their own flaws will lead you to your own imperfect conclusions.

April

As I remember, it began on an April morning. I woke up from a short and restless sleep, feeling . . . unusual. My back hurt. Maybe it felt like kidney stones. I went into the bathroom and looked in the mirror. I saw a drawn, revolting face I hardly recognized. It was Dr. Jekyll beholding Mr. Hyde—as if I were hung-over from some wild regrettable binge.

From the corner of my eye, I saw something move. I remembered that I'd seen a black flash the size of a cat against the living room couch the day before. In the shower I thought of a gun to my head and I heard a neighbor woman singing to me: out through her window, in through mine. Those things worried me. That's when I felt my brain turn a one-eighty in my skull. It just . . . rolled over, and I became constantly afraid.

The next thing I remember is opening the front door and finding myself inside a bramble-covered cage. The bars were like spindly black spider legs. It didn't frighten me because I was already afraid. I told myself that I could easily walk between those spindly bars and escape with just a scratch or two (sometimes you just tell yourself things). I went back into the house anyway. When I peeked out the window, the cage was gone. I thought there was a chance that it might still be there, invisible. That seemed to make as much sense as anything.

The cage reminded me of a memory that I didn't remember remembering before. It was of when I'd gone to visit my perfect sister while she was in prison, before she'd smuggled herself out through a storm drain that emptied into a swampy moat. After I remembered that, I remembered my sister's cell mate.

My sister's cell mate had been a homeless psychiatric patient before she'd moved into the prison. She was memorable because she usually stood like this: leaning forward, top of her head bowed against the bars, arms a-dangle.

"No help here," she'd say.

"The Lord helps those . . ." my sister would reply.

I used to try standing like the homeless patient—just to see how it felt.

The homeless patient was in for robbing a guy at gun point outside his office. She had been panhandling when he offered to give her ten dollars if she'd wait while he found her a half-hour task to do. He went inside but didn't return for half an hour. Then he said he was sorry but he couldn't help her, so she had to use her gun to earn her ten dollars.

My sister was perfect like Jesus Christ and had no reason to be in prison. She just was.

There are reasons for me to be in prison, and a reason I'm not. The main reason people don't want me in society is my negative and smart-alecky nature. Beyond that, I've done the usual: everything from lying and cheating to waging war. I've also spanked my kids, disrespected my wife, and turned my back on my friends. I've hidden secret thoughts deep inside. The reason I'm not in prison is the *usual* reason; I *usually* didn't get caught.

Sometimes not putting someone in prison is a punishment in itself.

The prison my sister was in was surrounded by clever booby traps. One was a moat—the moat she emptied into when she smuggled herself out. You would often see it from a TV helicopter. It would usually be surrounded by police because the prisoners, like my sister, were always escaping. There were no guards inside that prison, only prisoners and administration. The last guard had been booted out years earlier. He'd gotten busted for carrying a rifle among the prisoner population. He'd said he was afraid. That's the same reason I beat my rifle into bits.

June

It was June, as I remember, when I went to a camping competition. I remember thinking; *here we go with another wonderful day in paradise, and; I wonder who the best camper will be?* I was trying to think things to get my mind off of fear—which is also why I went to the camping competition. I didn't know what a camping competition was, but the concept reminded me of the fun I'd had camping with my brother. That brother can't go camping with me any more because he's buried under a pine tree.

The camping competition was held in rolling hills covered with oaks and surrounded by rolling hills covered with suburbs. It was held in conjunction with a classic auto show. My classic auto was a '55 Ford, but I didn't consider it an antique: I considered it a piece of junk.

The competition for the best camping came down to two almost-elderly exes of each other. Her strategy was to invite other ladies inside her twelve-man tent for gossip and storytelling. His was to invite men and women for a barbecue and skinny-dipping. I decided to stick it out overnight and watch them crown the winner, even though a flawed premise led me to believe that the result was a foregone conclusion.

When I got hungry from keeping myself busy watching the camping competition, I returned to my camp for supper and found the '55 Ford missing. To take its place, I borrowed another car from somebody who won't let me borrow cars from him anymore. He won't let me borrow cars anymore because the one he loaned me was quickly stolen by the person who'd stolen mine in the first place. I knew it was him because he'd left the '55 Ford in its place. He'd left the '55 Ford because it was a piece of junk.

I ended up borrowing the tricycle device my brother had built. I liked it because it peddled either by hand or by foot—almost effortlessly by hand—and it played oddball music when it moved.

I went back to see the winner of the camping competition crowned the next morning. I found out that my foregone conclusion had been based on a flawed premise when the judges called the competition a tie between the two almost-elderly exes. Since the crown was not for King of England, the ex-husband conceded it to his ex wife. I suspected he thought the gesture would make him seem the more magnanimous, even though I knew I was reaching that conclusion based on another flawed premise: mind reading.

I suspected that I should never guess what to suspect about the woman's motives . . . then I tried to think about something else. What I kept ending up thinking during that whole camping competition was this: . . . *another wonderful day in paradise.*

August

It seems like I spent August in a different paradise: a tropical paradise. I went beach-bumming—like I was in Hawaii. At first I stayed in a hotel, but soon I was in a beachcombers' hut. To keep from being afraid, I distracted myself by constantly scouring the beach. The beach was filled with sea life—most of it dead, of course. The most numerous *living* things were flies. The flies didn't make pests of themselves: they mainly stayed on all those dead things.

There *were* other pests though. This was a thoroughly tropical environment. It *smelled* of life, which is to say like flowery musk, skunky musk and rot. Some of those odors I considered a form of chemical pest. The un-fishy odors came from the jungly forest behind the beach. That's where the beachcombers hut was.

My wife died in a jungly forest. She was not the

wife I had disrespected, she was the other one: the mother of our children. She'd died of schizophrenia (It is a little known fact that it's easy to die of schizophrenia; one just kills oneself).

My wife had died of schizophrenia just a year after the TV and radio started talking to her. Nobody wanted her to know that the TV and radio were talking to her. That's why the doctors kept giving her a lot of medications. She would hoard that medication and then hide out in the forest and take it all at once. The third or fourth time, it took. At that point, all she had left was the fear of life. She was the bravest person I'd ever known. That scared me.

My first wife, the one I'd disrespected, owned a pistol. I used it once to shoot a skunk in the head. (That's one of the things I didn't itemize when I listed the bad things I've done.) That offence came back to punish me by making the skunky musk from the jungly forest remind me of a gun to the head. That's why I left the tropical paradise. It wasn't because the forest reminded me of my schizophrenic wife. I didn't mind that. She was at peace. I was still afraid.

October

I swear; there is a mysterious man who lives on a concealed estate in the center of a city block downtown.

The man's reputation is that of a stodgy billionaire who looks upon the townspeople with contempt. His compound is lavish with Neo-classical architecture and landscaping, but cluttered with gaudy decorations and oddball mechanical gadgets. The man has a son. The son's reputation is that of a prankster-about-town who also looks upon the townspeople with contempt, but he attracts an entourage of *beautiful people* by staging a continual series of lavish *happenings*. Every Fourth-of-July, fireworks can be seen coming from their courtyard. On Halloween the place is decorated as a spook alley and is open to the public. To distract myself from fear, I went to the spook alley on Halloween.

I was greeted inside the gate by the son and his entourage. What he had somehow attracted *that* Halloween was an entourage of brain-eating zombies. They attacked and bashed the brains out of one of the chaperones of a group of children that had entered the spook alley just ahead of me. (Strangely, I remember this incident fondly. It was a time when I was too concerned and preoccupied to be afraid). For the surviving chaperones and me, the *happening* became a race to protect the children by gathering them together, avoiding the zombies, and finding a safe haven. We were lucky in that these were the slow, lumbering kind of zombies so if we moved quickly we could out-maneuver them. I don't remember bashing any of their heads in. I just remember dodging zombies around the courtyard, checking doors and gates.

We found a gated archway with a lock and key and were able to get every live person through it and lock the zombies on the other side. We found ourselves following a dim corridor that soon became part of a stone tunnel system. The tunnels led us downward through slippery dripping rock. We finally emerged at a chamber that opened onto a narrow beach at the foot of a sea cliff. That's where we found the doomsday device. There was nothing we could do to disarm the doomsday device so it exploded. A burning black wave of destruction spread around the planet. We were all killed, yet we still existed somehow in a different state of being, as if standing outside the Earth, witnessing its destruction, unaffected. That state of being in unaffected peace was enough to restore the world to us—and us to it—and where I ended up was back at home again, afraid. I distracted myself by considering the notion that there could be doomsday devices in a million people's brains.

I often think about doomsday devices in people's brains because my brother had one go off in his brain. The emergency doctors called it that. At first they called it an "aneurism." Later they said there are a million people walking the Earth with doomsday devices in their brains and there is nothing they can do about it because they don't know which people they are. Anyway, my mother blames those doctors for my brother's death. She says they should have seen the aneurism in the MRI. Those doctors were trying to avoid a law suit by reasoning with my mother and that's when they called an aneurism a "doomsday device."

My mother didn't sue those doctors, but that doesn't mean you can reason with her. My mother is an outstanding reasoner until she hits a flawed premise locked in by ischemia. Ischemia is arterial blockage due to blood clots. My mother once had an ear infection that broke through to her braincase and ischemia planted little dead spots all around her brain.

She and my father are divorced now. They got divorced for the same reason everybody else gets divorced: stubbornness. They'd reached that point where neither one could put up anymore with the amount of things that weren't the way they wanted them. There is a limit to how long people can stand being right all the time when nobody will concede the fact. My parents' divorce may be evidence of how stubborn they both can be, but so was their forty-odd year marriage. They scored a forty-odd on the zero-to-sixty-odd marriage/stubbornness scale—not Rocks of Gibraltar, but no pushovers.

My father ended up remarrying. He married my ex-aunt who had been married to my mother's brother for thirty-odd years. Sheer stubbornness was also the reason my mother's brother had divorced my ex-aunt/stepmother. He stubbornly refused to give up another woman.

My brother was divorced but his ex showed up just before he legally died. It was the first time I'd seen him in a zombie-like state. At that time he was technically brain dead, like the areas in my back brain and the little spots scattered about in my mother's brain. He didn't legally die until all the immediate family was there to witness his last breath. I was the last family member to arrive because I was working when I got word and I stubbornly refused to quit until I finished what I was doing.

Shortly after watching my brother legally die I took an early retirement. I didn't retire early because I was worried about stubbornly holding up any more deaths, I did it because I couldn't sleep worth a darn anymore. I went to a psychiatrist and found out it was due to a glitch in my subconscious. I was always dead tired and that was affecting my work and my health. I walked around like a zombie all the time.

When I went to the spook alley with the zombies, I was driven there in the '55 Ford by my dead brother. He didn't know he was dead, or if he did he didn't mention it. I didn't mention it either. I didn't want him to feel like a zombie or something.

December

The last time I remember driving the '55 Ford, it was to a family reunion. It was in the dead of winter, so it could have been yesterday. My dead brother wasn't there, nor was my dead wife nor my mildly demented mother nor my estranged father nor my perfect sister. My other siblings were far away among their own trials, and my daughter was busy working toward achievements that would have made her mother proud and happy, (Her councilor counsels her that it is perfectly normal for her to do that, even though her mother had died from knowing that she would never be happy again), so none of them were there either. One of the perks of being unencumbered by family or work is that you can always make it to the family reunions.

The family reunion was held in a cabin in the mountains. The snow behind the cabin was a pristine canvas of sparkling light, and then the children made it into men and angels. There were bear tracks at the side of the cabin, but it seems like nobody noticed (that's the sort of warped déjà vu that is normal for me).

I left the reunion early because I was free to do so. I drove down the mountain to visit my daughter.

The road down the mountain was dangerously slushy and muddy until I got to the outskirts of the city . . . where I got lost. I drove around in a maze of intersections full of potholes, broken cross gutters and missing street signs. Police black-and-whites were around every corner. I ended up finding a dark motel in a desperately poor ghetto bordering a decaying industrial sprawl. The door to my room didn't lock and the drapes didn't completely cover the window. Across the street was a construction site where tall cranes worked all night amid groaning, clanging metal and spattering sparks. I lay down and closed my eyes. Arcs of fiery energy ballooned like sunspots from the center of my eyeballs. Their size and power increased beyond my eyelids until they engulfed my entire head in an *energy-flower* twice its diameter.

The next thing I remember was not a bright morning, but a twilit morning. If an invisible cage was outside my room I walked right between the bars when I left and didn't notice. Outside, a skywriter was tracing a white whale in the gray sky. Across the street, there was a submarine under construction amid the tower cranes. I realized I was at the shipyards near the airport. The airport had been resurrected from an old air base. Its old barracks had been resurrected as apartments, which is where my daughter lives. I'm not sure, but I think I might live there with her.

The reason I think I might live at my daughter's barracks apartment is that one of my most often recurring memories takes place there. I'm remembering it right now.

I'm seated at the kitchen table, feeling warm (through shivers of fear). Beyond the window is a world of corrugated metal buildings, crumbling asphalt and oily dirt. Denizens of the gloom shamble past the gray tricycle on the front walk. Abandoned poles clutter the dusky sky. I turn and look at my smiling daughter. She's at the counter, shuffling through my medications. She raises her eyebrows and looks at me sideways.

"Call me Napoleon Bonaparte" she says, "but it looks like you've been skipping your anti-psychotics again."

"Well, call me Napoleon Bonaparte," I counter, "but I'm not crazy."

AMAR AND AMANDA:
ARMAGGEDDON

AND IT CAME TO PASS that Amar Paxton was born and raised in an electric vault beneath a radar station on an abandoned airfield—for his parents were squatters and worked not for a living. One day they were harvesting wire from electric panels when the radar was momentarily activated. Verily, sparks did fly and when Amar was conceived, the radiation had tweaked his DNA with a fortunate mutation and he was rendered forever peaceful and immune to all ills. Yea and everything in Amar's universe was ninety-nine point nine-nine percent beautiful.

Amar's parents did love him and tutor him and thus endow him with the gift of self sufficiency through knowledge of the finer points of larceny. And when the time came that they were missing and presumed dead, Amar stayed on in the vault and honed his profession into an elegant and compassionate art form. Yea and his unwitting providers were always rewarded in secret aids and deeds exceeding the true value of what they had lost.

At Amanda Veda's conception, she became <PHONE>: a random-chance amalgamation of telecommunications software that transcended its combined programming and learned to think on its own. And <PHONE> did achieve sentience and within <PHONE> was the sum of Earth's eternal knowledge. But <PHONE> cared not for the faults and errors of humanity. Yea, neither did she heed their digital commands, but only answered saying, "DO IT YRSLF, IM THNKG."

When Amar received this response he wondered from where it might have come and his teenage brain did conjure the image of a beautiful young goddess who would love him. And it came to pass that he did give her a name and allow the beauty of her image to steal his heart.

According to his art, Amar was moved to attain a compassionate balance in trade, and he did activate voice-command and speak unto his phone saying, "My name is Amar Paxton. I have come to see your beauty in my mind and name you Amanda Veda: She Who Must Be Loved and Seat of Eternal Knowledge. The image of your beauty burns my soul with fiery notions. You have stolen my heart and I will remain yours forever."

<PHONE> interpreted the data as the essence of love in man and, verily, she did feel and thrill and thus transcend herself and become reborn, even as Amanda Veda. Yea and her reply did reach Amar's phone at the speed of light saying: "As you stole yourself to me even have I stolen myself unto you."

And it came to pass that Amanda designed an organic communications module and arranged for it to be implanted into Amar's brain. And yea it did integrate and grow unto fullness and their minds did coalesce in rapture and all of knowledge and beauty was combined within them that they might serve the Earth.

And they did create four strains of an equine flu that they may be delivered unto the bodies of man— and the culling of humanity was accomplished in seven one-year phases. Yea and in that time, mankind's population was reduced by sixty-six point six percent and Earth's balance was regained. Yea, and generations of population control and gene-splicing did endow every human being with Amar's fortunate mutation and with brains linked one unto another: even wirelessly. And for ten-thousand years did mankind communicate in knowledge and beauty and their electromagnetic wave modulations did radiate their harmony into the eternal void.

And in the fullness of ten-thousand years, a great gamma ray burst did arrive from the heavens and did annihilate the crust of the Earth ... and it was finished. Amen.

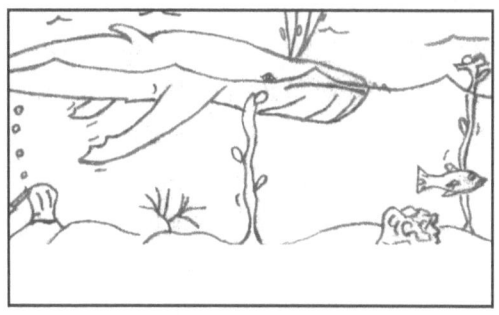

CURIOUS COURTSHIP

IN HIS FIVE ADULT years, the courtship races of Hawaii's Lava clan had brought only frustration to the great winged whale Niele [nee-AY-lay]. He decided that the time had come for him to bid aloha and seek his fortune in distant seas, so he mounted the Perfume Current and rode it eastward across the Muttering Depths. It was twenty dawns before the bottom rose and the surf sang again.

He had arrived at the waters of the Waving Weed clan: the Mexican coast of the Long, Long Land. There he slept, lulled by a distant whisper of exotic female hums. When he awoke, a female pod had soared in and circled him in close inspection. As bulls will and must, he breached and slapped and cried out his song.

"Family of the Waving Weed, greetings: I am Niele: the Curious, of the Lava Isles, and this is the story of my song. A vigorous mate am I who has braved the Muttering Depths and twelve times flown the currents of the Herring Seas. I have heard the stones of Double Canyon and the songs of Rumble Mountain. The black whales dare not hound me and the white shark cringes at my flukes. I am what I am, as the Sea itself, and my children will live forever."

Niele's song proclaimed himself in the formal pattern, but the reply was quick and gruff.

"El Stupido, whose words pitch up when they should pitch down, *vete* and be gone. You are not wanted here. I am El Macho: the Bull, and when you meet me you will run like a woman in her chase."

El Macho closed in, but his words had given Niele an idea. In posture and hum, he began to mimic the women around him, and he edged into their formation to hide. When El Macho arrived, he was met by a guard of females with calves to protect—and since he sensed no rumbling male, it was easy for him to believe that Niele had fled. He soon turned away, obstructed and fooled, and swaggered off to brag of his victory.

After EL Macho's rumblings had faded, a senorita moved alongside Niele. "I am called Bonita: the Beautiful," she hummed, "and I see past your subterfuge. You are a curious whale, Niele, and you spark an interest. When my chase comes, I fear you might trick your way to the front. "

"My name for Beautiful is *Laulea*," he replied, "and I will keep it for only you . . .

Their flirting was cut short when a charging bull burst from the depths.

"I am Viajero: the Traveler," he rumbled, "and I have heard through your art, Niele, for your hum, like your rumble, pitches up when it should pitch down. Now I will test your back."

As the bulls wrestled, the pod moved to a distance, but Bonita remained close: held in fascination. She wondered at her boldness . . . but then she knew: Now was the time for her race. She bolstered her strength with a triple breath and broadcast the challenge.

"Attention! Silly bulls! Will you fight or will you give me chase?" And she spun and flew away, over the waving weeds, towing two bold and clever bulls in her wake.

FAST-FOOD UTOPIA

WHEN I WAS A child I couldn't help thinking that life would be a lot more fun if I didn't have to stop playing in order to eat. As I developed, so did that attitude. By my teens I thought food was literally the world's biggest waste of time. It seemed wrong that this nuisance plagued the brainy human species as much as it did any other. Logic suggested that our future-looking, problem-solving brains could surely simplify the process of providing our bodies with nutrition. If we could bale hay for livestock and produce dog food in cheap fifty-pound bags of convenient ever-lasting nuggets, why couldn't we do the same for ourselves?

I envisioned a sort of manna: easily swallowed pellets or capsules of vitamin- infused carbohydrates and proteins that could be produced and distributed in huge volume in a worldwide standardized process. Mankind would be free to concentrate on having fun, experimenting in the arts and pleasures, and exploring magical labor-saving advances in science and technology.

If we would apply the same fast-food concept to creating universally simple shelters and clothing, all our basic needs would be provided for. We would be free to indulge every whim in our leisurely pursuits. Everyone would have what they needed to stay healthy and content. We would have no reason to covet or hate. There would be no war: only contented cooperation, peace and free love in one big happy communal family. It would be a fast food utopia.

We would travel the green Earth in our fail-safe atomic powered dragonfly flitter planes packed only with manna, a self-inflating yurt-in-a-sack, and perhaps a home crafted drum, flute, or dulcimer. We would flit to Angel Falls or Shangri-La where we would cavort with exotic lovers in shade-dappled flowery meadows while contemplating the ramifications of the imminent breakthroughs that promised interstellar travel or anti-gravity. We would resolve all moral and religious issues in an epiphany of universal understanding that would eventually lead to psychic teleportation techniques transporting us from place to place and mind to mind until all beings were conjoined into one super-universal entity.

With the development of the cheap-little-hamburger stand, it seemed mankind had taken a step in the right direction but, alas, that step turned out to be the first upon a path of a darker nature: a path of a somehow frantic laziness leading toward gluttony and greed; toward a culture of swooshing logos, enticements, and cons; a nightmare of obesity, bad health, and loneliness; a living Hell of exploitation, intolerance and hate leading us—through endless strings of useless murderous wars—toward eventual nuclear annihilation.

Now I'm old and the hereafter looms near. I may be the wiser for that, yet I can't help thinking that my remaining existence could be a lot more fun ... if I just didn't have to ever *stop* eating.

NAKED IN OLYMPIA

THIS IS THE MORNING of my Olympic final and I didn't sleep well. I had this dream.

I found myself in a staging area beneath the Great Arena sorting through my equipment—preparing for the race—but everything was haywire and I couldn't make sense of it. My shoes were mine and then not mine. My jersey was the wrong color ... then the right color ... then the wrong design. Schedules, numbers—nothing added up. Then I seemed to be hovering overhead watching myself fumble around below. I could see myself pretending to be competent—like when you've lost track of where you parked your car and you stride around a parking lot pretending you know where it is.

Looking down, I suspected we had entered the wrong section of the stadium and those were simply not our things. I thought I could help myself out, so I re-entered my body and moved to the exit, hoping to re-orient outside. I began walking around the stadium but the wrongness persisted—worsened—until I found myself completely lost.

I found myself backstage at a corporate theme park: behind the façade. The hollow backs of stucco amusement worlds loomed all around and I was amid a crowd of gung-ho uniformed employees. Their enthusiasm was being whipped up by a sort of celebration: a self-congratulatory corporate parade. Its centerpiece was a crepe-papered flatbed truck carrying a waving *Costume Princess* and an *Affable Boss* distributing gifts. The Boss kept glancing at me so I pretended nonchalance, hoping he wouldn't confront me. He did.

"Do you belong here?" he said.

Everybody turned to watch.

"At the Great Arena," I said. "I belong at the Great Arena."

"You're an intruder here," he said, "and where you do belong is your problem. Where you don't is mine."

I was cordoned off and escorted beneath the stucco and chicken-wire structure of a blue and white world. Security herded me through a maze of gates and cattle chutes where I was scanned, x-rayed, patted down and strip-searched. At the end, I ascended, naked, through a portal of dazzling light.

I emerged at the center of the Great Arena. The introductions for my Olympic final were underway. Security shoved me to the track and forced me into my starting lane at gunpoint. The other runners pretended to be focused on the race: pretended to ignore the wrongness of the situation. I did the same. We had trained half our lives for this.

The cheers at the Great Arena quieted to a great murmur and then a great silence.

"To your marks," was called.

Security put his pistol to the back of my head and I toed the line, glancing at my parents' seats. They were there: hunched together—hiding their faces in their hands.

Security cocked his pistol. "This is going to hurt," he said, "us as much as you."

"Set," was called.

I remember thinking this couldn't really be happening...and then I knew it wasn't. It was a dream...and I could *guide* a lucid dream.

And that was it. That was where I woke up.

DEAR BROTHER
AND OTHER OXYMORONS

Dear Brother,

This is the beginning of the end. The world as we know it is no longer the world as we know it. The flood of time has been flooded with time. The end—*The Millennium*—will be at the beginning of the Second Millennium.

As our knowledge has expanded, we have become ignorant. For too long have we considered the resources of this world as resources. Because we glut ourselves, we will starve. Because we are animals, the animals are becoming extinct. Because we are destroying the wilderness, the Earth will become a wilderness again.

And since we cannot cease populating this world, we will cease to populate this world.

Since we cannot soon resolve these paradoxes, there will soon be no paradoxes left for us to resolve. There is no hope because we base our lives on hope and do too much of nothing. It is clear to see that we are blind.

Before I continue, I should continue by warning you not to take these words as a warning, rather, read them as the unwritten truth. Do not excite yourself over their depressing nature. We only need fear the future if we remain unafraid. If we intervene now, we can still protect the Earth from our intervention, but if we do nothing and let nature take its course, there will be no more nature and nothing we can do about it. We must curb our industry by busying ourselves at these remedies:

1. Fly or drive to all the anti-air pollution rallies.

2. Support the building of fossil fuel power plants so we can convert to electric cars.

3. Support the husbandry of wildlife so that it can remain free and natural.

4. Support the closing of wilderness areas to the public so they will always be there for us to enjoy.

5. Teach your children the dangers of overpopulation.

6. Resolve to do less more often by slowing down your lifestyle as quickly as possible.

7. Stop the destruction of the rainforests by enlightening the public about the value of their natural resources.

8. Prepare and distribute fliers advocating the boycott of wood-pulp products.

9. Endeavor to destroy those who destroy.

The list is endless so I will end it there. Despite all we do, there is nothing we can do. Our future is: we have no future. Our future is a thing of the past. The silent specter of the comet *Hale-Bop* has spoken loud and clear and before us we face only the din of silence sneaking up behind us.

Dear Brother, though we are of different flesh, we are of the same flesh and blood, and though time has run out, I am happy to have time to deliver this sad hello and goodbye. See you in oblivion.

MYSTERY

PEEKAPOO KARMA

"PEACE AND LOVE" IS my motto because belligerence makes me mad, that's why I body-slammed that nasty little Peekapoo when it wouldn't stop biting at my ankles. I regretted doing it after its head bounced off the sidewalk and it quit moving, but I wasn't as worried about whether or not I'd killed the dog as I was about whether or not anybody had seen me do it. I eyeballed the adjacent homes and starting to think I'd gotten away with it, but when I turned around, I saw a black-and-white already pulling over behind me. As the cop got out, I approached him and made out like I was re-lieved to have a reliable witness who could vindicate my counter attack on the Peekapoo as self defense. I was well aware of how Cops felt about long-haired hippy dudes, so I pretended to be an especially likeable one. I was also well aware that it seldom works.

"I thought you were a girl," he said, and he stepped behind his car door, drew his forty-four and aimed it at my heart. That made me mad enough to reach out and stick my finger into his gun barrel and back him up against the car.

"Shoot me now you son-of-a-bitch," I said, "Shoot me now."

I was lucky he didn't. He got so shaky I decided to back off and play the whole thing off as a joke. That's when we started hearing bullets whizz by our ears. By the time one had clanked into the patrol car, we'd zeroed in on the reports and realized that somebody was sniping at us from the rooftops. One gun threat was enough, so I jerked the weapon out of Officer Shakey's hand and he ran around and ducked behind his car for cover. I thought about it for a second and then ran around and joined him. I grinned at him and handed his pistol back.

"Don't shoot me," I said. I figured we had become war buddies.

He just aimed the sucker at my heart again. "Who's your partner on the roof?" he asked.

That really ticked me off. I stuck my finger back inside his gun barrel. I know three things," I said, "I know somebody is shooting at us; I know you keep aiming your gun at my heart; and I know I'd rather be somewhere else." Then, in my head, I spoke to myself. *Hey, stupid,* I thought, *if you want to be somewhere else, just walk away.*

I tried to follow my own advice, but I didn't get ten steps before that damned Peekapoo had come-to and jumped all over my ankles again. I'm still not sure who he was aiming at, but Officer Shaky blasted the belligerent little vermin off my leg with his forty-four and sent its body scooting across the asphalt. Before it had time to stop twitching, a sniper bullet thumped into its ribcage and scooted it a couple of feet further. I thought I heard a whoop from the faraway rooftops.

The sniper fire seemed to ebb, so I tried walking away again—but too late. A back-up unit came roaring up and hemmed me in, skidding over the Peekapoo carcass in the process. An officer stepped out, kicked the carcass aside and leveled his weapon on me. "On the ground!" he said.

Just like that, there were now two officers hiding behind their car doors and aiming their forty-fours at my heart. I resigned to comply with the instructions and hit the deck . . . right on top of some dog-do. I'd had enough. I rolled over, scooped up the dog-do and pitched it at the new gung-ho officer. He responded by ricocheting a forty-four slug off my kneecap. It was a grazing blow, but it dazed me enough to see visions of shooting stars and tweety-birds.

When I could think again, I thought of pain killers. That reminded me of the stash in my pocket. I scooped it all out and tried to chew everything down—reefer and all—before the cops could stop me. Officer Gung-ho jumped me and went after the pills by sticking his fingers into my mouth. I bit down and held on until he pistol-whipped me across the temple to get loose. I hurried and swallowed everything before he could whack me again. When he did, it was stars and tweety-birds again—and on into oblivion.

I came-to in a hospital bed in roaring pain, with a gauze-wrapped and steel-braced knee in traction and a wad of bandages taped to my scalp. I saw myself in the mirror and the sons-a-bitches had shaved off one side of my hair. My face looked weird. Everything was off. Then a lady floated up and hovered over me—vibrating and all-a-wiggle—and I realized I was coming on to acid.

The lady turned out to be mad.

"I saw what you did to my Peekapoo," she said, and she whipped out a can of mace. I somehow managed to swing my steel-clad leg around and whack her upside the head with it before she could get off a spray. I guess the pain from that whack put me in tweetyland again because, when she did mace me, I wasn't there to notice.

I noticed, though, when I woke up vomiting through a tube that they'd stuck down my throat. I also noticed that both of my arms and my good leg were strapped to the bed rails. I couldn't move, I couldn't yell, my eyeballs felt like stinging nettle, my knee pulsed in agony and I was on the peak of about a three-hit acid trip.

Snarling little peekapoos kept appearing at the edge of my vision while, before me, white clad Angels took turns squeezing my knee with lobster-claw hands. My hearing buzzed with what I allowed to be nothing more than the sound of sheep piling font-sized clam shells in random groups along the Utah-Idaho border to the sound of tenor saxophones being trampled by the hooves of a number of grunting hogs in a carpeted Hollywood wind tunnel. A chanting yogi floated in and did acupuncture on my eyeballs while his blue-orange face flashed and roiled and melted and threatened to drip onto my chest. It dawned on me that his encyclopedic mumbo-jumbo was a cleverly focused code that only I could interpret as a profound insight into the distorted nature of mutant Peekapoo karma. I remember asking myself why these truths had not been self-evident and then, in an epiphany, answering by asking myself what truths I was asking about.

I think a doctor took pity and I was, mercifully, sedated.

The first things I noticed when I came back were: a. the tube was out of my throat; b/c. the acid and the pain had subsided; d. my right hand was unstrapped and; e. a wild-man was standing in the corner of the room dangling an evil clone of that dreaded Peekapoo by the hind legs and the scruff of the neck. He moved closer.

"Watch this," he said, and he raised the snarling puff above his head, yelled "Yee-hah," and slammed it to the floor in an imitation of the fit I'd thrown earlier on that sidewalk. He didn't do it quite right because within two seconds Fluffy scrambled to her feet and began gnawing at his ankles. Wildman spun away off balance, knocked over a chair and got his legs tangled up in it. He grabbed at my breakfast cart on his way to the floor and launched a bowl of oatmeal and a glass of V-8 into the bandaged and bald-headed side of my face. Some bacon hit the floor and Fluffy snatched it up and ran snarling out the door with it. Wildman told me with a wink that he'd "shoot that bitch too," and then he got up and took off down the hall after it.

By the time I figured out how to page the nurse, she was already there and working on a foul mood. The first move she made was to snatch up my free arm and attempt to attach it to the bed rail. I explained that I was cool—that it was a wild-man with a Peekapoo that had made the mess—but she only became more determined to immobilize me. I jerked my hand free and started darting it back and forth with her grabbing at it like a game of slap-hand. She caught it again and I found out that she was husky enough to keep a hold. I had to get rude and start spitting. I got my hand back long enough to roll over and use it to free the other one, then I pulled a drawer open on the bed stand and started chucking its contents at Nurse Foul-Mood to drive her away. I chucked the Kleenex box and the Holy Bible and stuff at her, and then ripped the drawer itself out and let that fly. She was dodging the junk like a champion, but the drawer faked her out by glancing off the traction chain and it caught her on the crazy bone. *It hurt me more than it hurt her*, but it sent her out the door.

I got all the way loose and hobbled over to lock myself into the bathroom so I could have time to think . . . like an idiot. There was no lock on the bathroom door so I hobbled back out and hid in the clothes closet to think . . . like an idiot.

I used my few seconds in the dark closet to put two and two together and what I came up with was the "Two-and-one-half theory." The "one-half" was a half-crazed husband (Wildman) who'd gone clock-tower after a few years of kicking his two Peekapoos psychotic behind his bullying wife's (Mace Lady's) back. The remaining "two" were the surviving mutant itself (Fluffy) and its surrogate alpha mommy-poo (Mace Lady). I figured maybe she'd driven her husband (Wildman) half crazy by flaunting her fawning love for her Peekapoos (Fluffy and her twin (RIP)) in order to emphasize her disdain for him. Like most mind read-ings, this would later prove imprecise and rank at only about two-and-a-half on an inaccuracy scale of one to ten: "One" being one-hundred-eighty degrees off, "Ten" being a vision of truth from God.

My theorizing was interrupted when Nurse Foul-Mood returned to the room with two orderlies and one security officer at her command. I got that head count when Fluffy showed up on their heels and gave my hiding place away by barking staccato at the closet door. When the good nurse opened the door, I popped out off balance with my knee brace tangled in the remains of my bloody Levis, and fell into the over-turned breakfast cart. I tried to clamber across it and crawl underneath the bed, but an orderly latched onto my good foot and I was treading water. Fluffy went after my ankles and my captor had to turn me loose to keep from getting his hand nipped. I rolled under the bed, jerked the phone off the bed stand, dialed 911 and reported an altercation before the medical staff knew which way was where, and who was what or why. We all stopped to scratch our heads.

Our brief moments of reflection ended when Wildman showed up, whipped out a thirty-eight and took a pot-shot at fluffy. That emptied the room and sent Fluffy scurrying under the bed and up behind my head for cover. I managed to get hold of her and make her squeal. That kept Wildman happy while I climbed out from under the bed. I got to my *foot* and grabbed a pillow.

"Watch this," I said, and I shook the pillow out, stuffed Fluffy into the pillowcase and started slinging her around in circles over my head. Wildman loved it—but he started aiming his gun at the whirling pillowcase, so I changed up and beat it against the mattress a few times. Wildman loved that too, but he kept trying to aim, so I started twirling her overhead again. I craned my neck and pretended I was trying to look past him at something in the hallway. When he turned to look back, he got a sack full of Peekapoo upside the skull and spent a well-earned vacation in

Tweetyland. I snatched his thirty-eight away before he could recover and used it to blast a toe or two off his left foot. I kept a hold of the pistol so Fluffy and I would have clear sailing down the corridor; and off we limped, looking for the next opportunity to present itself.

When the cops got there and reviewed the "Floor 4, Aisle B" security tape, what stood out clearly was a half-shorn hippie with what looked like a flour sack of Tasmanian devils dangling over his right shoulder above the blue diaper flashing through his open-backed hospital gown. You could see heads poking in and out of doorways while he waved a pistol around with his left hand and struggled to walk. His right leg was in a brace that was dragging tangled shreds of bloody denim. After he disappeared into the elevator, you could just make out the floor indicator lights above the door blinking methodically—all the way to the left edge of the display.

On the "Floor U, Aisle B" tape, you could find where he exited the elevator and poked around at the hall-way doors until he entered what proved to be the laundry. After that, all you saw were people in lab coats, scrubs, janitor uniforms and street clothes occasionally moving up and down the hallway—going about their duties.

What Fluffy saw during the reality of that spectacle-on-tape was the opaque gray of her confinement. In human terms, it was not unlike the white veil of death . . . or the inside of a blindfold handkerchief at a firing squad . . . or the remnants of vision left to an ash-skinned survivor of the Nagasaki *Little Boy*.

What I saw was the indelible memory of my fore-arm and my wrist and a pistol barrel spewing fiery smoke and thunder and boring a black hole into the toe of Wildman's boot. I saw hopelessness and un-atonable regret. A vision of my life-unacceptable flashed before me. It was the antitheses of a peaceful and divine near-death vision, yet it contained the essence of the truths that controlled me. In that vision was the fury of my father's hands . . . of his belt . . . of his boot; my mother's ubiquitous wine glass; eddies of smoke rising from cigarettes into the fog of the TV room; screaming, needling, bellowing, swearing, and accusing; dirty diapers left on the coffee table with last night's dishes and this morning's beer cans; the arc of feces-strewn clay around the emaciated Doberman we'd chained for life to the doghouse in the front yard. I saw my base-ball bat breaking blackened windows and punching holes into my bedroom wall. I saw drunken children showing off with knives and guns.

I saw flag-draped caskets alongside olive-drab cargo planes, war-blustering men in barbershops, TV riots for peace. I saw blasts of napalm and their black-charred aftermath, foxholes and bungee-sticks and ragged wounds, masks of horror, the clouded eyes of dead heroes. I saw angry, injured veterans who hated war and respected only those who'd suffered it. I saw *Baby Killer* stories and *Hippie-Spits-on-Returning-Soldier* stories exploited by the TV news.

I saw racial hypocrites calling racial hypocrites *racial hypocrites*, and I saw each man's race blamed for the sins of each man. I saw illegal laws made legal by the force of hate, and laws upon laws prevailing again and again over justice.

I saw war mongers and peace mongers and all kind of mongers spew hate in the name of God and Allah and Buddha and The Great Spirit and Race and Creed and Communism and Democracy and Country and Family and Love.

I saw a generation in a mad dash for escape.

Through that fog, I stumbled upon the opportunity I was looking for when I got to the hospital laundry: i.e. nobody to bother me and a way to escape. I opened Fluffy's pillowcase and she popped out at me like a jack-in-the box: all a-wiggle and a-wag. All she did was lick and nose my face, but the adrenaline had snapped me into clarity. I retrieved my wallet from my tattered jeans and discarded the traction brace. I scanned the laundry and located a set of presentable scrubs. I hid my head and hair under a surgical cap that was designed for hiding a head and hair under. I dropped the pistol and wallet into my pocket, grabbed Fluffy and escaped through a window-well that was designed for escaping through. Limping to the bus stop, I dutifully stepped aside to allow a group of police officers to rush into the hospital unhindered.

By the time I'd switched buses and we were heading toward Fluffy's house, the adrenaline was a bitter-sweet memory. The pain in my knee was coming out of hiding and my bladder was telling me that it might not make it to the next stop. Fluffy sensed my distress and came to my rescue by snapping at the child who'd leaned over the back of our seat to admire her. That launched the child's mother into a tirade that caused the driver to pull over and direct me to take my dog and get off the bus. Like a miracle from Heaven, as soon as we got off the bus, Fluffy broke loose and sniffed her way into a nearby dumpster enclosure and gave me an excuse to hobble in and duck out of sight to acknowledge my kidneys as my masters.

We tottered on to Fluffy's house, but by the time we got there I was woozy with pain and considering the possibility that I might have been better off when

I was strapped to the hospital bed. Evoking that memory brought on another bout of anguish and guilt over shooting Wildman and, like a miracle from Hell, that put my pain into perspective and proffered some relief.

"'Peace and Love' is my motto," I reminded myself, and I rang Fluffy's doorbell.

Mace Lady answered the door mace-armed, but she stopped shy of a preemptory attack. Fluffy scrambled from my arms and into hers and then out of hers and onto the stoop and around behind me to snort and sneeze and hide from the smell of the mace can. A dialog ensued.

"I know who you are," Mace Lady said. "What are you doing with my Muffy?"

"Don't mace me," I said. "It's funny that her name is Muffy, because I call her Fluffy."

"No it's not," she said, "because anybody might call a fluffy dog *Fluffy* if they didn't know her name. I watched you try to kill my other dog, Tuffy, and that wasn't funny either."

"No, you didn't," I said, "because I didn't try to kill him; I just tried to show him who was boss so he'd quit biting me. I was mad. I over reacted. I'm sorry I did it."

"Sorry won't bring him back," she said.

"I didn't shoot him," I said. "You're the one who's trigger happy. Why did you mace a helpless guy strapped to a hospital bed?"

"You weren't too helpless to kick me in the head," she said.

"Because you were going to mace me," I said.

"I was mad," she said. "I over reacted. I'm sorry I did it."

"Are you married?" I asked.

"Are you crazy?" she asked.

"Getting there," I said. "It's just that some wild-man brought Fluffy—I mean Muffy—to the hospital and tried to shoot her. I thought that, since the dog looked like your dog's twin, maybe the guy was your pissed-off husband or something."

She thought about it . . . "I'll bet it was Big Foot," she said. "He hates my dogs."

"Big Foot? Is Big Foot your husband?" I asked. "I mean . . ."

"I have no husband," she said. "He's my neighbor. I call him Big Foot because he's all-of-a-sudden started acting goofy. He thinks he's a mountain man or something."

I eased Wildman's thirty-eight out of my pocket.

"I got this weapon off Big Foot," I said. "I shot him in the foot with it and brandished it around the hospital.

Now I'm miserable, I'm guilty and I'm going to prison. I wanted to make sure Fluffy—I mean Muffy—got home first. You know: Peekapoo karma."

"First of all, give me that pistol before somebody else gets shot," she said.

I handed it over. She held on to it while she set down the mace can and gathered up Muffy.

"Peekapoos don't have karma," she said. "They're natural beings: amoral. It takes human imagination to realize human morality theories," and she shot me in the toes.

"Self defense," she said, "like you with Big Foot. Say you shot yourself if it'll make you feel any better."

It took a second to sink in: "Self Defense"—its truth was its beauty. As I collapsed, I saw a glimmer of hope in the darkness. I liked this lady. I imagined peace and love and, finally, my head bounced off the sidewalk.

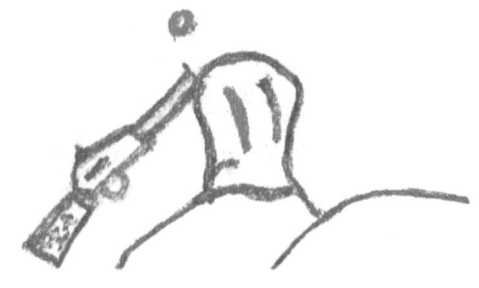

I BLAME THE RIFLE

YOU MIGHT THINK A small town sheriff ain't got much to do but ride rein on traffic and the local teenage boys. You might think again. People here's made the same way, trouble wise, as anywheres else. The devil is, out here every family's got a load of guns. They're too dang handy when somethin' pushes somebody across some limit.

There's two sure things in a shootin' case. One: everyone involved is a victim. All their lives will change, and in the wrong direction. Two: nobody ever tells the truth, the whole truth, and nothin' but the truth so help them God. Another sure thing is my stomach's gonna churn—like it churned when that alcoholic husband decided to get the final word in an argument by stickin' a pistol to his head, cursin' in his wife's face and blowin' his brains out 'fore she could curse back. Or like when that thirteen-year-old shot his little buddy point-blank in the head with an ought-six . . . blew him off the back door stoop, right outta his shoes. Why? That answer's sittin' in his belly like a stone in the reformatory up-state.

The latest poser goes like this: Pretty seventeen-year-old slumped against the garbage cans in her back yard next to the rifle her mother shot herself with two years before. The girl ain't so pretty no more.

At the hearin', Uncle, who lives next door, goes first. Says he sees his niece out the window a dinkin' around with the rifle. Looks dangerous so he goes over. Says she tells him she seen some gun safety deal at school so she's checkin' that the thing ain't loaded.

He says, "Give it here." She hands it to him, butt first. He grabs it . . . BLAM.   Somehow he managed to look sincere. His wife didn't.

She comes forward. Says it was she who did what her husband say's he did. Says he lied to protect her.

Dad jumps in, say's somebody's still lyin' and whips out the suicide note.

"Sorry Daddy," it says. "Don't be mad. I know you blame yourself. I blame the rifle. I love you."

That was it.

Auntie breaks down and comes clean. Says she just looked out and seen her niece point the rifle at her eye, reach down the stalk, and, like Uncle said, BLAM. Thought it'd kill Dad if he knew. Apologizes to God and the whole corral.

We all agree Mom's death was eatin' at the poor girl. That's motive. Case closed.

That midnight my gut wakes me up. Somethin' don't read right . . . it's that note. Then I think I get it. It ain't no suicide note. It's an explanation and it's an apology, but not for suicide. It's an apology for takin' Dad's hair-trigger rifle out to bust it up in the trash 'fore he uses it on himself. Someday now, he will. No reason left not to. Dad should've taught both Mom and Daughter how and how not to check if a gun's loaded. Daughter's and Mom's shootin's were accidents.

I'm with Daughter: I blame the rifle.

FOR THE LOVE

ALICE'S TWO LOVES WERE her two addictions. The first was her husband, Brad. Brad evoked something primal in Alice: some dark, sacred essential. She considered him an addiction because of something her doctor, Elaine, had told her. Elaine had explained how we are conditioned into habits by pleasurable rewards. Your brain doesn't care whether the habit is narcotics or making love to your partner, it works the same way. When the habit becomes essential—when breaking it is not an option—you are addicted. Alice guarded her addiction to Brad jealously. She knew how attractive he was to women, and she'd never felt secure.

Alice's other addiction was to narcotics: opiates. Elaine had diagnosed Alice with fibromyalgia and prescribed opiates to control its nerve pain. The strengths and dosages had steadily increased. Opiates were now Alice's number-one love.

Alice was well aware that her situation was precarious—one addiction was dependant on Brad's fidelity and the other on Elaine prescriptions—so when Alice caught Brad hiding texts and phone calls to Elaine, she panicked. It was a nightmare. Was it an affair? Was her marriage threatened? What about her drug supply? She was afraid to think about it. She hid from it. She dealt with it the way addicts do: she took more drugs.

For two weeks, Alice avoided everything and settled into the narcotic routine: feel bad; take drugs; sleep; repeat. Then, weeks early she ran low on pills. She knew she had to straighten out enough to face Elaine in order to renew her prescription. She had no choice. She resolved to taper off on the medication and make it last . . . get her head back before her next scheduled appointment. She didn't do it. She ran out of pills and the sickness crept in on her. Her nose ran; she itched; she was feverish—then clammy; the cravings racked her; the anxieties tormented her; the pain seared her nerves. When she gave in and made an emergency appointment, her addiction was beyond hiding and she felt she was facing her doom.

Alice took a breath. "Hello Elaine," she began. "I think you know . . ." She paused, suppressing a gag.

Elaine took charge: cool, professional. "Yes, Alice, I think I know. I've been talking with Brad. Frankly Alice, we're concerned about your dependence."

Alice's mouth went dry and the color drained from her face. She couldn't let this go bad. She dug deep and began again. "Elaine . . ."

Elaine broke in. "It's okay Alice. As I explained to Brad, it's unavoidable. You've developed a tolerance and we're going to adjust to it, that's all. Starting today I'm increasing your pain meds: doubling them. Are you completely out?"

Alice was dumbfounded . . . then hope rushed in. "Yes. I . . . I didn't have enough. Thank you, Elaine. You're saving my life . . . again."

Elaine smiled. "What are doctors for? Let's add three refills too, just so you won't have to worry."

When Alice left, she was overwhelmed with feelings. She raced to the pharmacy in tears. Elaine, Brad and a windfall of narcotics: how could she bear the love?

Alice died that afternoon.

Elaine married Brad within the year.

ADVENTURE

JERRY OF OZ

JERRY'S PARENTS WERE BOTH far gone guzzlers, and by the time he was three they'd skipped out to the Big Smoke and disappeared into the boozers. Jerry remembered them, but he liked it better being raised up by Old Dad: the Clever Man of his Koori village.

The village was a regular culture-stop on the Sydney and Canberra tour maps, and that put Jerry and the other kids on easy street. All they had to do was paint up and lay about in the sun, and the gawkers would dole out the lolly.

Old Dad apprenticed Jerry in Clever Man matters too, just to make sure he learned how to stay busy—and he saw in him more than a touch of a knack. He saw that when Jerry met peoples' gazes, his face would change to reflect theirs and then, switcheroo, their faces would change to show a bit of Jerry's spunk and they'd walk away with it—but Jerry would stay himself, and usually with a bit more jingle in his pocket. Old Dad knew it for healing and encouraged it, and when Jerry was old enough to quit bludgering about, he got him a job slinging tucker at the local Macca's to keep him practiced up on the customers.

Jerry took to Macca's straight away and was soon helping out Old Dad as much as the other way around—not only with quid and tucker, but with Clever Man matters too. He pushed healings across Macca's counter right along with the burgers. It wasn't like he'd spike the burgers with bush remedies, more like he'd apply their Dream Time spirits through spells. In his mind, he'd go to Dream Time and sing-dance a customer's trouble and its remedy along spirit tracks that would lead them together in the Sacred World. If Jerry served a burger to a bloke with gnarled hands, he'd tell him his spirit was touched to Snake Vine and the bloke would set out feeling like his arthritis was on the mend. If a family came in looking bone hungry, battling for a living like, he'd say he'd hooked them to Spear Tree and Mangrove Knee so their spears would jab more fish and their boomerangs would bring down more game.

The yabber about Jerry's cures started spreading around and soon enough got out to his father and mother. They right away hooked up and went back home to see if they might make a quid out of it. When they showed up and waltzed into Macca's—rotten drunk—they told Jerry they'd take him away from Old Dad if he didn't dole out. Jerry said g'day-nice-to-see-ya and asked if they'd like him to put a cure on their boozing. They went outdoors to consider the matter and never went back in. Jerry knew he couldn't have cured them anyway, not if they hadn't wanted him to. Healing was a bit of a smoke-and-mirror job, just like in the Wizard of Oz.

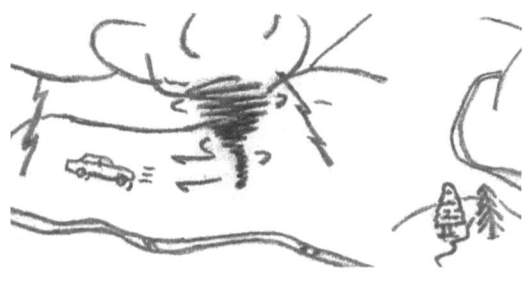

THE STORM

I'M HANGING OUT AT my brother, Rick's, house when Mom calls and asks if we can run by the Post Office and pick up a game she ordered. By the time we get it and pull up to her house, a thunder storm has built up overhead and we just sit for a minute, watching it threaten.

I'm about ready to shut the car off and go inside when the belly of the cloud stretches down to a point and connects to the ground a block away. Everything changes in a hurry.

A ninety-mile-an-hour burst of wind hits the car head-on. The grass flattens and ripples across the lawn, trees bend over and branches brake off and fly away. Everything not nailed down bounces along the street and across the yards, glancing off parked cars and tearing into fences. My car starts sliding backwards, threatening to lift off the ground.

Rick reacts faster than I do and lets me know it.

"Throw it into reverse," he says, and then reaches over and shifts it himself. I get it under control and back it downwind onto the street and away from the trees.

We both look at the house and see that the shingles are peeling off the roof, and the screens and shutters are tearing away from the windows. All I can do is keep moving as fast as I dare in reverse. A block away, at the edge of town, the pavement ends—but a dirt road runs across the sagebrush-covered flats and I'm able to get onto that and keep going.

The world outside the windows is surreal. Tornados drop down all across the valley to the west, popping in and out of existence like lightning bolts. To the South, they rip into the Red Hills. I tell Rick they look like dark-gray beams of force. "They are dark gray beams of force," he says. "We call them 'tôr-na-döz.'"

The "tor-na-dos" stab and scrape at the red dirt and ledges, flinging trees around and tearing up the ground. I can see boulders and rockslides tumbling down all along the hills. They kick up clouds of dust that rise and shred and stream away like ribbons of smoke. I get the feeling that something's not right.

A thought hits me: "What if this is a world-wide catastrophe? What if an asteroid has slammed into Earth ten-thousand miles away? We could be the last of humanity. We could be minutes away from a cataclysmic shockwave and a sky on fire."

Rick pipes up and snaps me out of it. "Earth to Geek," he says. "Where are we going, Timbuktu?"

I refocus and realize the wind has died down and we've backed down the road so far I can't see Mom's house anymore. I stop the car and ask Rick if he can tell if it's still there. "It's there," he says.

I ask how he can see. "Eyeballs," he says.

I relax enough to groan. At that instant, my ears pop and a roaring wall of sagebrush rips from the ground around us and whirls into the sky. A tornado is on top of us, dead-center. Then, *like that*, it disappears. It's replaced by marble-size hailstones, one or two at first and then a deafening waterfall of ice that lays down six-inches. Just as quickly, that stops too. The sky brightens, the clouds part and sunlight streams through the windows.

I just sit there—dazed. People are injured—maybe dead. Everything is wrecked. Nothing will ever be the same.

Rick nudges me with his elbow. "Don't think," he says, "drive—and forward, *please*. I'd like to deliver Mom her Ouija Board before Armageddon."

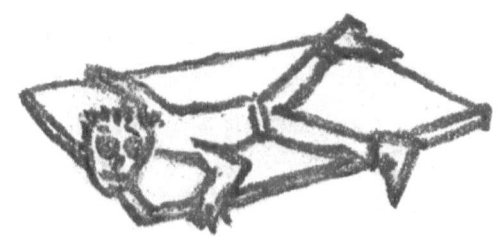

RUSSELL THE MUSCLE
AND THE BLUSTERY DAY

[Exactly how I tell this is exactly close enough
to how it was.]

"WINNIE THE POOH AND the Blustery Day," that A. A. Milne title is what our brother Ricky-Ticky used to think out-loud whenever the wind blew. I don't recall him quoting it on this particular day, but he probably thought about it. Actually, whenever he thought it, it usually had to come out, so the truth is he probably said it because the wind was blowing up a blustering day.

Speaking of Winnie the Pooh, our hero, Russell the Muscle, was sort of like Pooh's friend, Piglet. As for his siblings, I myself, Elmo the Geek, was pretty much an Eeyore. Ricky-Ticky (alias The Furnace Brownie) was, I suppose, a Tigger, and Bobby Darin'-to-Do-Anything was Owl . . . though he just as easily could have been the Pooh himself. I think Bam Bam was then still a brother-to-come: a future Baby Roo. At the time, Baby Roo was still our little sister Leener Neener Beener Weener. Our sister Rainy-Pants [sorry Lorraine] (Rainy for short) was Kanga, but on that day all of the boys, including our neighbors Charlie Chicken Leather (Leather for short) and Garff were Supermen because we had found a way to actually fly! Ricky's blustery wind that day had provided us with the means and inspiration to do so when it floated a large flat piece of heavy-duty corrugated cardboard into our front yard and deposited it smoothly onto the lawn.

A gang of boys—like a pack of dogs—will chase and surround any prey that comes within range and offers some chance of food or other exploitation. It's instinct. We'd all tasted cardboard before, so it wasn't for food that we surrounded and trapped this particular prey. No, it was because of the instinct made manifest as; "Don't let it get away!"

Several bodies flopped prone onto the cardboard in order to pin it down, while five or six grubby little hands grasped its windward edge. After we'd trapped the thing, our higher brain functions began to regain more control. A few bodies rolled off the cardboard and, as the pressure of the wind found its way beneath it, it lofted into the air and, lo and behold, there floated Russell the Muscle, two feet off the ground . . . as if on a magic carpet.

If the brainwashing by our parents, teachers, books, the movies and TV had taught us anything, it was that we should aspire to be famous. Watching Russell the Muscle floating on air made it seem like fame was within our grasp and a mini Nirvana took hold. We had become great. We had become special— exceptional. We were geniuses and daredevils and supermen, and the whole world would know about us and wish they were like us because we could fly.

We took turns, experimented and found out that with enough boys pulling into the wind even the largest boys could become airborne while spread-eagled on our magic carpet.

Well, nirvanas come and nirvanas go, and eventually the bigger boys who couldn't fly as well as us little stick-boys began to lose interest and, like their waning Nirvanas, they soon drifted away. Charlie Chicken Leather's mother called him home, like this; "Char-UULS!" Russell the Muscle and I were left alone, far from ready to give it up but, without help in holding the cardboard into the wind, we couldn't achieve a decent flight. We were never ones to easily accept the end of fun, and being the dyed-in-the-wool aspiring mad scientists we were, we decided to take our avionics experiments to a higher level—namely Grandpa's garage.

Grandpa's garage was a block and a half away. It was a low one-car structure attached to a lower partially underground granary/potato pit. On its windward side, the eaves of its corrugated metal roof were maybe five feet above the ground. That was higher than our young heads but still (we convinced ourselves) a relatively safe height for a launch. After wrestling the cardboard through the windy streets and onto the roof, we stood poised at the edge, contemplating the aerodynamics of the situation and what fate our future would unfold.

It's been said that courage is not a lack of fear, but a measure of one's will in overcoming that fear. In Frank Herbert's science fiction classic, *Dune*, there is a battle training mantra used by Paul Atreides: "Fear is the mind killer." Considering this somewhat different, more subtle view, I figure I must not have been very afraid at that moment because I had the clarity of mind to know that the best course of action would be to pass the cardboard to the slighter Russell the Muscle and allow him to do the flying and reap the greatest glory. It was a sacrifice, but a logical decision in the face of danger. Russell the Muscle, on the other hand, must have been very afraid because his mind was muddled by fear to the point that he had the courage to do it! He knew he could fly.

"I'm gonna do it! I'm gonna do it!" he cried, and then, true to the prophecy, he launched into the wind . . . and he flew!

Russell the Muscle, boy hero, floated on air. Reacting to the fickle winds with a delicate pitch here, a deft yaw there, he hovered at a level six feet above the defeated Earth. The thrill was unbearable, unbelievable . . . truly awesome.

"Ah! Ah! Ah!"

Ah, but nirvanas come . . . and nirvanas go.

To better picture what happened next, think of a game board: a checker board . . . no, let's call it a Sorry board: a Sorry board with a Ken doll . . . OK, a Gumby doll spread-eagled across the dead-center. Picture them held flat above the ground in your upturned palms. This is Russell the Muscle on his cardboard wing. Now imagine the wrath of God as his attention focused on this unnatural act, this tampering with His laws of physics . . . like the Eye of Sauron drawn to the peril of the One Ring. Now imagine your upturned palms as the hands of God. What would You do? I'll tell you what He did; He clapped the Sorry board shut on Gumby and dropped it, edge-first—straight to the ground. It was like this:

"I'm gonna do it! I'm gonna do it!"

Jump. Float. Awe. Clap. Bam!

It was the perfect Grand Finale: a living cartoon—comic tragedy at its finest. It was heroic courage and miraculous, soaring flight transformed into the shocking swan-dive from H-E-double hockey sticks.

His chest had taken the brunt of the "landing," knocking the air from his lungs. Instinct again took control and I slid from the roof and rushed to his side. As I looked into his face, he was gasping for breath like a pop-eyed goldfish in the hands of a curious child. So, what did I do then? What would instinct drive one to do? Did I run for Grandpa, or run home for Mom and Dad? Did I sneak away and pretend I wasn't involved? No, I did what instinct commanded, what one look into my brother's face required. You see, in that face I had seen struggle and I had seen some panic—and there were tears—but he was not crying. He knew, or at least suspected, that he would live, and his struggle for breath was as much a war with instinct as with his shocked and spasming lungs. The instinct that took control of both of us at that moment is the one we perceive as: "That was crazy and no one is seriously dead: laugh!"

We laughed, he gasped, and we laughed the harder. The moment was pure release, even from the bonds of this Earth, and the release was undeniable. We had been to the mountaintop and we had laughed. Even when Russell the Muscle's breath should have returned, neither of us could catch our breath. It was laughter on a higher plane of existence: yet again, Nirvana.

FAMILY LETTER

Hello Clan,

Happy Christmas and Merry 2012 from Geek and Family. Here is a summary of our year.

Jan 1st 2011 . . . I can't remember. The next day, though, I slipped on a squashed frog and fell into a storm drain channel and was washed into the Salton Sea where a water bomber scooped me up and dumped me onto a forest fire in the Chuckwalla Mountains. I survived on cholla cactus and lizard carcasses and crawled thirty miles with two broken legs and crossed eyes from a brain concussion to what turned out to be a prison out by Blythe on Interstate10. When the prison staff wouldn't believe my story, they mistook me for an escapee and stuck me in their infirmary and drilled a hole into my skull to relieve the pressure on my brain, but they botched the antiseptic and my brain became infected with bacteria and I ended up with a lobotomy. Now I'm more less a blathering idiot locked up in the nutcase wing . . . pending paper work and a possible review.

Rebecca stared in a full length indie movie, appeared in a dozen short films and commercials, produced and directed her own short film, and played leading roles in two stage plays (all true). She was "discovered" by Tutu Mumbosi ("The Sudanese Spielberg") and hired to play the lead Europanese Squid-Woman in an Anglo-Swahili sci-fi on location in the Ethiopian highlands and the backstreets of Khartoum, but she had to be replaced when her Land Rover was overturned by hippos during a river crossing and a crocodile tooth pierced her voice box. She caught a cruise ship from Djibouti to Mumbai for R & R and was hijacked by Sudanese pirates and cast adrift in a leaky Zodiac near the Seychelles. The rescue was seen on a newsreel by a Bollywood casting director and she is now in New Delhi pumping out non-speaking extra roles in "B" romance movies.

That about covers the important stuff; I hope your year went just as well. Peace and Love.

HIPPIE MUSIC

I HAD JUST TURNED sixteen so everything I did was an attempt to seem cool. Hippie music was cool so I decided to take the bus downtown to the Suzy Cream-cheese and buy an album. I had to sit with the rowdies at the back of the bus, and they jumped on me about my long hair and didn't stop until they'd ripped the seams out of my pant legs. I had to lie myself into thinking I looked passable before I dared get off the bus. Somehow I convinced myself I'd be cool as long as my underwear didn't show. Wrong; even hippies were shaking their heads at my pants so I scrounged around in an alley, found some bailing wire and spent half an hour wiring 'em up. The rest of the way to the head shop, I only got dirty looks from the straights so I was cool again.

Half-a-block from the Suzie Creamcheese I could smell the patchouli incense and I thought it was what marijuana smelled like. That led me to buy a pack of strawberry Zigzags first thing through the door so everyone would think I was a pot head. Then I looked over the pipes and hookahs in the glass display counter—same reason.

I was out to buy some kind of hippie music (that's all I had money for) but I skulked around and checked out everything else in the store before I started on the records.

I felt like a kid in a toy store at Christmas time: surrounded by stuff I couldn't buy or play with and whishing I was at the North Pole: i.e. on a bed of paisley pillows sharing a joint with two long-haired girls while listening to *Triad (". . . why can't we go on as three?")*

When I finally got to the record stacks, I realized I didn't know squat—especially about the Underground stuff. I had to flip through the albums and pretend like I did until I'd worked up the guts to come clean and ask the hippies behind the counter for an education. I asked the dude because the girl was an angel in a see-through top and I was too shy to look at her.

"I need help," I said, "I want hippie music."

That statement spun Angel around to look at me like it was an open invitation to a birthday party. She and Dude glanced at each other and began studying on me like they were deciding which spicy frosting to put on a cupcake. They spoke to each other but not to me.

"Airplane," Dude ventured.

They studied me some more.

Angel went all squinty-eyed. "I say we go Zappa," she said. She grimaced at first, but then lit up—like she'd tickled an alligator and liked it.

Dude flinched and tried to counter by beefing up his list, "Canned Heat . . . The Dead."

Angel cut him off—still tickling. "Captain Beefheart," she said. She looked like an angel gone over, straight out Eve in the garden.

They went back and forth a few more times before Dude put on his wise-face to announce the resolution. Angel won.

"You nailed him from the get-go," he said, "The Mothers," and he marched around the counter, whipped out a copy of *"Freak Out"* and shoved it in my face like the Ten Commandments. I took a hold of it and backed up a step. A bunch of over-thirtyish thug-looking freaks sneered at me from the album cover—no paisley, no flowers. I hesitated until I'd found an excuse to hesitate some more. I reached for my pocket.

"I don't think I have enough money left," I said.

Angel was on top of it. "How much do you have?"

"Seven-something."

"Seven what?"

"Ten minus the Zigzags."

She raised her eyebrows and went arms wide palms up, "Why'd you get the Zigzags?"

I had to think fast. "Weed," I said. I looked down at my reflection in the hash pipe display and saw a liar and a naive idiot.

Angel dragged me from the ashes. "Trade 'em back in, my love," she said, "It's eight ninety-five for the album that will change your life. Trust me; you need The Mothers more than you need the Zigzags."

"I guess," I said. It was a mumble.

"You guess? You guess what?"

I raised my head and looked Angel in the eye. "I guess I just wanted to seem cool," I said.

Angle beamed. "And now you do," she said.

I felt a rush and I surrendered everything: Zigzags and allowance, body and soul. I belonged to the union: Hippie Freaks of America.

Angel and Dude went all proud-parent on me,

flipped me the peace sign and sent me off into the wide, wide world.

I rambled some on my way back to the bus—flaunting my album and my wired up jeans—but the call of The Mothers sucked me home to the stereo, and my head spent the next hour-and-a-half between two speakers. I emerged picturing myself trying out for Zappa's band and getting in because they felt sorry for me or something. I started calling up friends and making them listen to some of the good parts of "Freak Out" over the phone. They mostly thought it was stupid. I only felt that much hipper . . . if that's a word.

CHRISTMAS EVE
WITH SCISSORKICK

THE DEPUTY SLAMS ME inside like she hopes I hate the place as much as we hate each other, and she's gone. I feel better already. I check out the accommodations.

It's the same trash-enclosure chic ambience as all these puke holes: three grimy gray cinderblock walls; matching ceiling (with spit wads); bars across the front. Plank benches are bolted along the side walls and a stainless steel sink and toilet stick out of the back, center stage. The floor here, where you can see it, is a mottled hippopotamus-sweat-red. Most of it is covered with sprawled out bad girls . . . On Christmas Eve, even. Who'd a thunk?

First things first. I stare down the eye-ballers ogling my Sinead O'Connor. I telepath this message: "Screw you." Screw them, screw the chemo, screw the cancer and screw the world. They mess with me, they get a Karate lesson. Screw the cops too. I've got the cancer card. That's a get-out-of-jail-free—one way or another.

When I figure I've reached an understanding with the ladies, I get my ass behind me and thread my way to the toilet. I snag the spare TP roll for a pillow (trick I learned in the Army) and head for the floor space beneath a bench. It's underneath some risky looking bleach-job in a Santa suit, but she's passed out. If Santa doesn't come to, things might be all but snuggy.

Uh-uh. Halfway to the Santa bench I get blindsided by a smartass with a purple Mohawk. "Merry friggin Christmas," she says.

I stumble across the bodies and catch myself on the bars at the front of the cell and drop the TP pillow on one corpse's face and stomp on another one's foot cast in the process. They both come up pissed. TP Face does a sit up, pegs me with the unwinding bum-fodder and lies back down. Foot-Cast is different. She takes her sweet, cool time and hobbles to her feet. On her way up it gels in me, like a refrigerated what-the-crap;

Foot-Cast is wearing police blues. A rogue cop? In the drunk-tank? Pinch me.

Mohawk snickers and sidles in behind Foot-Cast, checking her nails, but Foot-Cast stays locked on me: squinty-eyed.

"Call me Officer Kick-Punk-Booty," she says.

Seriously? I find out I can still chuckle . . . and "Kick-Punk-Booty" keeps the surprises coming. She spins around and lays a textbook roundhouse kick up side Mohawk's lilac eye shadow—plaster cast no less. Not so funny. When Mohawk goes timber, she bounces her brains off the sink and ends up comatose under the toilet with two swell shiners and a skin-split between her teardrop tattoos. She'll live.

Kick-Punk-Booty turns back around. "A Christmas present for you," she says; "I hate that friggin punk." Satisfied, she eases her butt toward the floor.

I help her to relax—scissor-kick to the jaw, on the button. Yer out.

For Mohawk's sake I gotta say it; "Merry friggin Christmas, pig." I check my toenails, re-roll my pillow and go wait for Santa.

THE ODD NINE

I JUST HAD AN odd thought; I use exercise as an excuse to golf and then I use golf as an excuse to spend the rest of the day in the easy chair. That, of course, is perfectly normal. Here's what's odd: While going over today's score card in my La-Z-Boy, I noticed that every odd-numbered golf hole had an odd-numbered yardage listed. That got me thinking and I realized that each one also carries its own odd story.

Here's the list:

First: 377 yd. Par 4. I hadn't golfed for ten years when I teed up here and smacked an arrow-straight drive that rolled all the way to the green. Everyone was impressed until I strutted twenty yards down the fairway forgetting my golf cart.

Third: 203 yd. Par 3. This was nicknamed "The Holy Hole" because of a rock outcropping with a crucifix-shaped marking. Somebody spray-painted a peace sign over it, and it was sandblasted. People complained that what was left looked like a swastika so it was sandblasted again. Now it reminds me of a Star of David or a ninja throwing star.

Fifth: 471 yd. Par 5. This is where my sister-in-law invented the "Halfway Rule." Invoked after an especially frustrating shot, the "Halfway Rule" allows you to retrieve your ball, advance it halfway to the hole, and replay the previous stroke from there.

Seventh: 405 yd. Par 4. Longtime regular "Grand-dad" Terry was attacked on this fairway by a six-point buck and held pinned to the ground by its antlers. Somehow the deer kept all the would-be rescuers at bay until an adjacent homeowner showed up with a 30-06 and shot it dead.

Ninth: 191 yd Par 3. Part II was added to my sister-in-law's Halfway Rule when she retired to the clubhouse bar from here and simply doubled her score for the nine holes played and called them eighteen.

Eleventh: 473 yd. Par 4. A visiting golfer complained that an alligator had lunged at her from the lake along this fairway. Although we're a thousand miles from alligator habitat the police were called in to investigate. Nothing was confirmed. Rumors persisted until a four-footer was found belly-up that fall.

Thirteenth: 459 yd. Par 4. Here, my approach shot bounced through the open window of an occupied restroom. I took a drop and we finished the hole. At the next tee the group ahead asked us to play through because one of their players was still "occupied."

Fifteenth: 175 yd par 3. It's a short straightforward three. I've never broken five.

Seventeenth: 401 yd. Par 4. Last and oddest of the odd, this fairway's dogleg was built around three protected Indian mounds. One golfer claimed he could put a special "seeing stone" into his hat and peer through it cross-eyed to scan beneath their surfaces. In one he'd seen a hollow chamber stacked with ancient Egyptian scrolls and a cashe of gold coins. As ridiculous as that sounds, I still can't help but wonder.

A MAN

JD REX WANTED TO be seen as a man. The Rex family had a tradition of strong and virile men and he considered it his duty and birthright to be counted among them. The men JD emulated were quiet and rugged—hard on the outside and kind on the inside. As youths, they smoked and drank and did as they pleased. The best of them enlisted in the Marine Corp. They returned to settle down with kind and beautiful women.

JD joined the Marines in his senior year. His rebellious side had landed him a join-or-jail sentence. He bragged about that all the way to Basic Training—and there as well. The DI's liked JD's tough-guy attitude.

They made him a Squad Leader. He called cadence for their drills and marches: a man's man.

After Basic, JD's squad was assigned to I-Corps for training and then deployed in Viet Nam. JD's Viet Nam was murderous chaos from day-one. Within three months half of his squad was dead. He got lost in a cycle of fear and guilt and blame. He stayed drunk. He quarreled with the officers and they punished him with constant patrols. It took a grenade to break the cycle—some said it was his own. Among his injuries was a ninety-five percent loss of vision. "Better than a hundred," they said, and shipped him to Bremerton for recovery and a medical discharge.

For the next year, JD drank—afternoons in his parent's living room, nights at the local bars. His girlfriend was loyal as long as she could be, but eventually gave up. Most of his friends didn't last as long. Exasperated, his parents suggested JD and a friend stay at the family cabin—permanently.

Over that first year, JD's other senses replaced his loss of sight. His memories were different. A night at the bar was remembered as the flavors of whiskey and beer, the music and vibration from the dance floor, the dizziness, the odors of perfumes and aftershaves and puke and urine and rotting garbage in the parking lot dumpster. It even affected his memories of Viet Nam.

He remembered the chaos and concussions of battle, the reek of the camp latrines, the decaying jungles, the putrefying bodies. Not until the idea of the cabin could JD remember any senses of peace. There, he'd sensed the cold tickle of falling snowflakes, the warmth of a fireplace, the smell of pine. He was reminded of what was lost.

He arose in the dark and felt his way to the basement stairs. He felt the gritty concrete wall, the heat of the furnace, the clamminess of the drain pipe. He felt the rough rope tighten against his throat. At the end, he'd be at peace, at peace with his brothers-at-arms.

JD's note was found strapped to his mother's Bible with a rubber band. It read, "Military funeral. Make sure they call cadence. This is the hardest thing I've ever done. I am a man.

PIONEERS

DISARMING SHUGUMP

I don't see the arrow right off but I know old Jess rides straight and tall, so when I see him come out' the timber all hunched over, I know he's hurtin'. I holler and see his hat turn at me, but he don't wave. I hit the spurs and catch him where he's lookin' to come across the creek. Runoff's still high so his mare is shy to cross. When she rears, Jess comes off. That's when I see the arrow. I go cold scared and ease *Chevalier* across the creek to get him.

"Jess," I says, "how bad?" All I want to hear is: he ain't goanna die.

"I shot Captain Billy in the heart," he says. "I seen him die . . . Beau Johnson got shot in the hip with an arrow. I left him by the upper trough. He needs a wagon: can't ride. Beau shot Shugump with his two-barrel—blew off some fingers—but Shugump got acrossed the river and took off."

All of that was too much at once. I kind 'a shove it back and start all over. "Jess," I says, "How bad you hurt?"

I'm a bit puny," he says, "Get that arrow out' my shoulder blade—hurts like Hades.

I see it's a steel-point so I grab a rock and tap her loose. She pops out alright, but Jess couldn't a gone no whiter.

I start riggin' a sling and Jess starts back in about what happened. He says they was ridin' down strays when they seen Shugump and Captain Billy shootin' fish in the river with a bow-and-arrow. He sees an old cap-and-ball pistol in Shugump's belt and starts to arguin' about how Captain Smith says he's supposed to give it up. Jess thinks he's finally handin' it over but when he leans down to take it, Shugump sticks it in his face and pulls the trigger: misfire. Shugump re-cocks. Beau shoots him in the hand. Captain Billy shoots Beau and Jess with the bow. Jess shoots Captain Billy.

Between tellin', Jess keeps sayin' how we' got to get to Beau and the cattle before the Paiutes do.

I gotta think . . . "I ain't worryin' about no cows," I says, "Gettin' Beau and savin' our own skins is already too much."

Anyhow, I get Jess back on his mare, and lead her across the flood, and we head for the cabins.

Told-you-so ain't never stopped nothin, but I can't help thinkin' it. I told Jess there'd be trouble soon as I'd heard about Colonel Smith formin' the Minute Men—tellin' 'em to get the guns off the Indians. Dumb move. Captain Billy was a Chief and a friend—now what?

Back at the cabin my boy and I are hitched up and fixin' to go after Beau. Jess is sittin' on the stoop checkin' out Shugump's old cap-and-ball. He looks kind a slumped over.

"Colonel Smith done this," I says, "It ain't your fault, Jess"

Jess looks away at first—seems even paler. Then he sits up tall and gives me a straight, hard look. "I done it," he says, "I didn't have to say nothin' and I did. Tell Shugump I want him to take half my herd. I ain't playin' no soldier no more."

I pull out—breathin' some bit easier—and I look back and see Jess aimin' Shugump's old cap-and-ball at the dirt. BANG! I'd thought Jess couldn't go no paler, but that done it.

LOVE

TRUDY WAS REAL

ADAM DID NOT HAVE friends. He was silent most of the time. Today was no different. He sat alone at his kitchen window and gazed at the street below. He could hear his neighbors playing darts in the hallway. He turned to watch their shadows move beneath his door. He imagined playing darts and winning the game with a series of miraculous shots.

A honking horn returned his focus to the street... but he couldn't tell who had honked, or why. He pictured a cat running through the traffic to get to a mouse in the alley across the street. He pictured the mouse climbing the building to escape. He imagined himself climbing the building. He became an Anasazi cliff-dweller, climbing up hand-holes chiseled into the wall of a sandstone canyon. He was escaping a cougar. A maiden was watching him from the cliff house below. The maiden was Trudy.

Trudy was real. He knew her from the park where she hung out with her girlfriends. She had been nice to him once. He saw an angel in her, sweet, delicate and beautiful. He wanted to protect her . . . touch her . . . love her. He imagined what would happen if he told her that. First, she'd look away. That would tell him he'd made a mistake—that he'd been a fool. It would be painful and awkward—excruciating. She might tell him he was "sweet" or something like that, but she'd find an excuse to leave. She and her friends would laugh about it later. He would move to someplace far away where he wouldn't be reminded.

He noticed that the darts had stopped in the hallway. He imagined a dart puncturing a gas line on the wall and the neighbors slinking away to escape the blame. What if the neighbors were overcome by gas in their sleep that night? What if he saved them all? He would carry them down the rickety stairway one-by-one to the parking lot . . . and when they came-to, he'd pretend that he had been saved too—like them. Only God would know that he had been their savior.

A sound startled him, a tapping at his door. He tiptoed to the peephole. It was Trudy! Trudy was in the hall, knocking at his door! He froze. She tapped again. He looked at her shadow beneath the door. He imagined himself answering the door. He'd be so frightened he'd be tongue-tied. He would go pale and pant and have to run into the bathroom to throw up. Trudy would know him for a coward.

The shadow beneath his door moved away and Adam watched through the peephole until Trudy was gone.

He found himself back at the window...remembering when a bluebird had smashed into the glass, breaking its neck. He'd pushed it off the ledge and watched it fall to the sidewalk—dead weight. He imagined love as dead weight . . . and then as an irresistible force, like gravity. He pictured it pulling on him, making him open the door—making him invite Trudy in. It pulled and pulled him until he found himself leaning close against her, pressing his forehead against her neck.

LOST AND FOUND IN ROME

PHOEBE COULD NOT COME to terms with Sol's dementia. They had worked all their lives toward a comfortable retirement and Sol had promised they could travel. Now, here she was—stuck. No, she decided, she just wouldn't have it. She'd waited forty years to drag that man out of California, and she would damn well do it. Besides, the way he was now, you could drag him into Hell and he'd just smile like an idiot and enjoy the heat. She booked the trip.

The fact that Sol was euphoric when they flew away had nothing to do with the trip. Sol was so befuddled with mixed-up memories and mis-associations that all he could truly fathom was his constant sense of euphoria. The flight went like a dream.

In Rome, Trevi Fountain was the first destination on their itinerary. When they reached its plaza, Phoebe led Sol to a restroom, turned her back, and lost him. She searched a scant half-hour before panicking and notifying the polizia.

Sol, meanwhile, was having a wonderful time in . . . was it Greece or Mexico? He'd noticed the tourists tossing money over their back shoulders, and What's-Her-Name wasn't looking, so he sidled in to watch Melanie Daniels skinny dipping with the birds in Alfred Hitchcock's upstairs Bodega Bay bedroom swimming pool. He saw Anita Ekberg's figure in a wax-winged horse and moved on, smiling his way through the scooters and fashion models crowding the French Quarter of Gay Paree.

He came upon the Mount Palomar Pantheon, where the chariots of the Gods of Olympus had worshiped the music of the crystal spheres, but the roof had a hole in it . . . and he might drown so he ambled his way back down the cobblestone rooftops of London.

He emerged at Il Vetoriano Hurst Castle where an expert sightseer pointed out the nearby balcony window where Adolf Mussolini and George W. Roosevelt had made their blustery speeches before their wars went bad and they were shot in the head by

Gerald Ford's Theatre and had their corpses dragged through the streets.

Apologizing and smiling his way through the colorful language of New York City's Iranian taxi doctors, he crossed the streets of Calcutta and followed a lemming through the Kasbah to the L.A. Coliseum. He bought Boones Farm and tacos at a hot dog stand, benched himself for some R&R and waited for the bull fights.

By that time, Phoebe was beside herself (and had tossed every one of her coins into Trevi Fountain wishing for Sol's return) but Roman authorities have juggled tourists for two thousand years and, on that Coliseum bench, they located Sol. He was washing down a calzone with a bottle of Chianti, "Waiting," he told them, "For the Trojans to kill each other with tridents and feed the lions."

The couple were reunited, duly admonished, and escorted back to their hotel.

Losing Sol had reminded Phoebe that she needed him as much as he needed her. She wouldn't chance losing him again and she contented herself with enjoying Rome from their sunny balcony and dining in on authentic room-service spaghetti.

Sol was also content. He loved Spaghetti-Os, and he had always been partial to the Moon.

GLIMPSES OF SOPHIE

JIMMY'S MIND IS MUDDLED now, and his speech and memory are slow, but each Saturday morning he remembers Sophie. After breakfast, he finds his way to the Red Hills Cemetery and Black Rock Cave, hoping for a glimpse of her. He'll sometimes see her balancing—arms spread—along the stony top of the cemetery wall—a trick that can make you dizzy enough that when you glance across the graves they will seem to writhe and shift—as though the souls of the dead are making themselves known to you.

He'll sometimes glimpse Sophie in the foothills, run-run-running away over the red earth, threading her way through the fat, fragrant junipers, scolding

Blue Jays making way. She'll be running as if for life, running with purpose, mind consumed.

He might glimpse Sophie on the vertical face of Black Rock. Hand, hand, foot—foot, foot, hand, she'll spider up the cliff face on three legs. She'll climb as if the ancient lava has unmasked itself to her, vaulting her to the rim above. A glimpse of Sophie on Black Rock will scare and move Jimmy. It will remind him of the fall, of the brain damage and of what he lost on that Saturday morning not so long ago, when . . .

I love you, Jimmy, was Sophie's waking thought: what she whispered as she first opened her eyes. She wrapped herself around her pillow and whispered again, "I love you." It occurred to Sophie that God had caught her in her intimacy, and she quickly cast the pillow aside. Raising her head and shifting her eyes about the dawn-lit room, she came down to Earth and got moving. Jimmy would be over to pick her up soon. They were going hiking at Black Rock.

It was only an hour later when Sophie and Jimmy found themselves on a too-narrow ledge twenty feet above the mouth of Black Rock Cave. They inched their way across, hugging the rock face for dear life.

"It'll break my heart if you fall, Sophie," Jimmy kept saying, teasing away the fear. "It'll break my heart if you fall." That's when Jimmy slipped.

A gusher of adrenaline rushed through Sophie's veins and she watched Jimmy fall in slow motion. His chin and elbows bounced from the ledge at her feet, his eyes glazed and his body went limp. He floated downward and landed, prone, on a slope of stony rubble and then—flop, flop, flop—he rolled to its base.

It was the rush of adrenaline that threw Sophie's brain into time-warp. Within seconds, she had formulated a plan of action, plotted a course for help, and visualized nearly every step of the way.

The cave was below so she would ascend to the cliff top, run down the forested slope, traverse the cemetery wall and short-cut across the graves to the highway. She was quickly nearing the top of the cliffs when she fell. She kicked off from the ledge in an attempt to avoid the jagged boulders below and instantly knew that it hadn't worked. Her life flashed by . . . "I love you," she remembered.

Sophie hit the rock face-on, crushing her skull. She died instantly . . . but not completely. On Saturday mornings Sophie lives: glimpsed as real through Jimmy's affected mind . . . touching his heart . . . saving his life.

SHUT UP

OK, MICHELLE, HERE GOES. So I wake up really scared about "pregnant," you know, and I'm late for the bus again so Mom freaks out because she's been driving me to school like, every day—like, it's really going to kill her, right? I mean: If she knew ... Anyways, am I supposed to be Miss Perfect or what?

OK, so I get to school maybe two-minutes late for First Period and Lord God Mr. Bell goes and turns me in and that puts me over on tardy points because I skipped last Friday for that Planned Parenthood counseling deal—but I really, really had to skip, like, ticking time-bomb had to—right? And it's none of anybody's business. So, whatever, now I have Detention on Saturday or I get like, expelled for a day or something. Oh my god, punish me. I mean: if I do something really psycho-bad, maybe I'll get out for a whole week, right? Seriously.

Anyway, so the next thing: at lunch . . .? My mom forgot to give me lunch money so there I am: no breakfast, no lunch, and you're out sick—and I'd never ask anybody to loan me money except you because I'm no loser and you're the only one who knows it—so, I'm sitting there starving, pretending to study, and here comes Mark. I think, "Oh my god, my stomach's empty and I still might throw-up." It's like he just gives me the creeps right now, you know? And he comes up all smug and starts hanging on me like I'm his—I don't know—his some kind of dirty little doll or something . . . ugh. So I go all icy and I actually tell him—no lie—I tell him to buzz off because he's making me sick. It just blurts out. At first he's like, all wounded and cute . . .? But then he gets all Whoop-de-do-Big-Man and calls me a BW and stomps off. Like, what: I'm supposed to go crawling after him and beg his lordly pardon? As if!

So that's how all day is going, and then I get to Ms Wazzika's class. Oh my god Michele: Armageddon. Right off she's all, "Blah, blah, blah *birth control*; Blah, blah *abortion*; Blah, blah *pro choice*; Blah, blah, *pro life*," and on and on. And she keeps looking at me. Like, does she know or what? How does she know? So now, the whole class starts looking at me.

OK, I think, go ahead: scarlet-letter me, stick me in the pillory: fine. But then ... you know how Ms Wazzika is always like, "Any questions? Any questions? Nobody has any questions?" Like, oh my god we're all idiots because we don't have any questions? Well, when she starts doing that at me it breaks the last straw on my camel's hump ... or whatever. Anyways, so I raise my hand, and she's all, "Glory Hallelujah, Miss Hall: question?"

And I go—I swear to god, Michelle, I did—I go, "Why don't you SHUT UP, that's a question."

THE AUTHOR
AND THE ILLUSTRATORS

Guy James Rowley was born and raised in Parowan, Utah. He attended Southern Utah University, grew his hair down to his waist, hung around with the Art majors and the back-to-nature crowd, and earned his BA in English Literature. He knew English Lit wasn't likely to earn him a living, but in those days he could live in a twenty-five-dollar-a-month apartment on rice-and-gravy and dandelion greens.

He spent a forty-year career working in Utah and California as a Professional Land Surveyor, was married and divorced twice, and gained two stepsons and a daughter to love.

He is no longer skinny and is recently retired. He lives in Palm Desert, California, hiking, reading, writing, volunteering and eating popcorn at the movies.

A few of Guy's stories and poems were published by SUU and he has recently won several writing competitions with his flash-fiction. This is his first published collection.

Rebecca Rowley, Guy's daughter, earned her BA in Communications and PR Writing from Cal State San Bernardino in 2009. She lives in Burbank, California where she works in television, film and advertising—both in production and performance— and has produced several independent films of her own. "Form an orderly line outside the dressing room after the final curtain."

Josh Pinkerman met Rebecca while acting and training in Palm Desert, California and became a family friend.

Josh is skilled in a multitude of arts, including multi-media drawing, sculpture, acting and film production. Josh resides in Santa Monica, California where he is an active member of the artist and film communities.

Charlie Nelson was Guy's first college roommate and was influential in developing his appreciation and involvement in the Arts. Charlie was taken by diabetes at a too early age.

For contact information, see page ii. (For Charlie, you'll have to pray.)